The Mighty Movers

Sidney Levitt

Hyperion Books for Children
New York

Text and illustrations © 1994 by Sidney Levitt.
All rights reserved. Printed in Singapore.
For information address Hyperion Books for Children,
114 Fifth Avenue, New York, New York 10011.
FIRST EDITION
1   3   5   7   9   10   8   6   4   2

Library of Congress Cataloging-in-Publication Data

Levitt, Sidney.
The Mighty Movers / Sidney Levitt — 1st ed.   p.   cm.
Summary: Moving men Fred and Ted tackle the tough assignment of
moving a stubborn ghost to a new house.
ISBN 1-56282-421-X (trade) — ISBN 1-56282-422-8 (lib. bdg.)
[1. Ghosts — Fiction.]   I. Title.
PZ7. L58245Mi   1993   [E] — dc20   92-54869   CIP   AC

The artwork for each picture is prepared using
watercolor and pen and ink.
This book is set in 18 point ITC Garamond Light.

To my parents, Libbie and Al Levitt
—S.L.

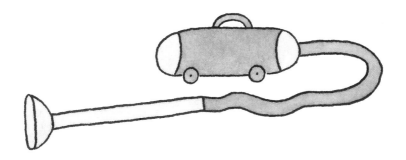

Fred and Ted were movers.
On the side of their truck
was a sign.

It said,

THE MIGHTY MOVERS

Big or small,

we move it all!

Once, Fred and Ted moved
a family of polar bears
to the North Pole.

They also moved a statue
of a giant foot.

They even moved
a five-hundred-pound gorilla
who helped them change
a flat tire.
"We can move anything!" said Fred.

One morning Fred and Ted

sat in their office.

The phone rang.

Fred picked up the phone.

"The Mighty Movers," he said.

"Big or small, we move it all!

Can we move a *what*?

Sure, we can move a ghost.

We can move anything.

Your address is 114 Cabbage Street?

We will be right there!"

Fred hung up the phone.

"We cannot move a ghost," said Ted.

"Ghosts are scary."

"I am not scared," said Fred.

"We can move anything."

Fred and Ted drove to the address
that they had been given.

It was a big old house.

Ted rang the doorbell.

Two rabbits opened the door.

"Hello. We are the Quimbys,"
they said.

"Where is the ghost?" asked Fred.

"He is hiding in the house,"
said Mr. Quimby.

"His name is Hamilton,"
said Mrs. Quimby.

"We want him to come and live
in our new house."

"Did you ask him?" said Fred.

"Yes," said Mr. Quimby.

"But Hamilton loves

this old house. He does not

want to move."

"Is he a scary ghost?" asked Ted.

"No. He is a very nice ghost,"
said Mrs. Quimby.

"But he is in a very bad mood,"
said Mr. Quimby.

"Can you make him move?"

"We can move anything,"
said Fred.

"I hope so," said Mr. Quimby.

"We really miss Hamilton,"
said Mrs. Quimby.
"Our new house is too quiet
without him," said Mr. Quimby.
The Quimbys gave Fred and Ted
the address of their new house.
"See you later," said the Quimbys.
"Good luck!"

Fred and Ted went back

to their truck.

"We have never moved a ghost before,"

said Ted.

"I know how to do it," said Fred.

He got a big fishnet

out of the truck.

Then they went into the old house.

"I wonder where he is," said Ted.

"Shh!" said Fred.

"You have to sneak up on a ghost."

"OOOOH! GO AWAY!" said a voice.

"That must be Hamilton!"

said Ted.

"Hamilton!" called Fred.

"We want to talk to you."

"NO WAY! GET LOST!"

said Hamilton.

"Where is he?" said Fred.

"It sounds like he is upstairs,"

said Ted.

Fred and Ted climbed the stairs.
Suddenly Hamilton whizzed
down the banister.
Then he disappeared.
"Yikes!" said Ted.
"He is fast!" said Fred.

Fred and Ted looked for Hamilton
in every room of the house.
They could not find him.
"He disappeared," said Ted.
"I know he is here somewhere,"
said Fred.

Suddenly they heard,

"Ha, ha, ha!"

"It is Hamilton!" said Fred.

"He is in this room!" said Ted.

They looked all around the room.

Hamilton was not there.

CRASH!

A light bulb fell to the floor.

"What was that?" cried Ted.

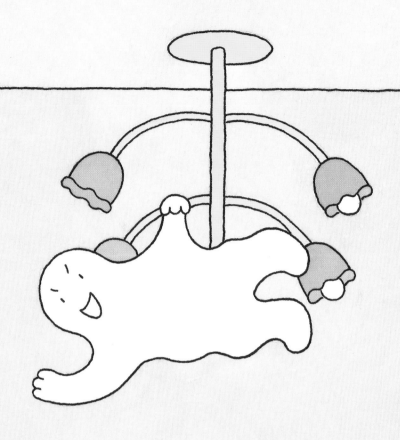

Fred and Ted looked up.
There was Hamilton
hanging from a lamp
on the ceiling.

"You turkeys will never catch me!"

said Hamilton.

"Quick, Ted!" said Fred.

"Get the net!"

Ted climbed onto Fred's shoulders.

He tried to catch Hamilton

with the fishnet.

But the net went

right through Hamilton.

"You guys must be kidding!"

said Hamilton.

He picked up the fishnet

and threw it over Fred and Ted.

"Help! We are caught!" said Ted.

"Get us out of here!" said Fred.

"Ha, ha, ha!" said Hamilton.

"I caught a couple of big ones!"

Then he disappeared again.

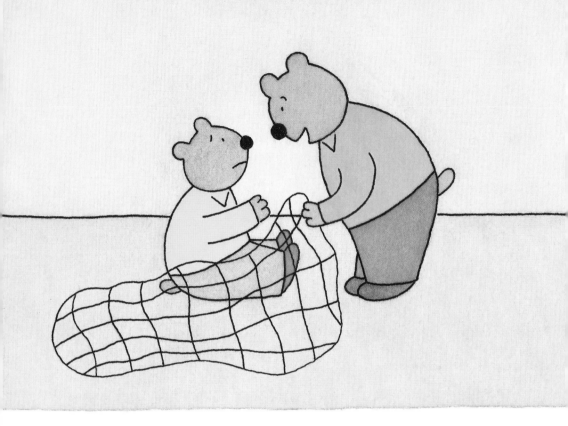

Fred and Ted got out

from under the fishnet.

"What do we do now?" asked Ted.

"I do not know," said Fred.

"We will never catch him," said Ted.

Fred thought for a moment.

"I have an idea," he said.

Fred ran to the truck.

He came back with

a vacuum cleaner.

"That will not work," said Ted.

"Hamilton will just laugh at us."

Fred plugged in the vacuum cleaner.

"Hamilton!" called Fred.

"We give up! We are

leaving now!

Good-bye!"

Hamilton appeared in the room.

"Good-bye, Mighty Meatheads!" he said.

Fred turned on the vacuum cleaner.

He pointed it at Hamilton.

"Ha, ha, ha!" said Hamilton.

"You cannot catch me!"

Fred and Ted chased Hamilton

around the room

with the vacuum cleaner.

But they could not catch him.

Then Hamilton pulled the plug

out of the wall.

"Oh no!" cried Fred and Ted.

Hamilton took the

vacuum cleaner cord

and flew around and around

Fred and Ted.

He tied them up together.

"Hamilton! Stop!" cried Fred.

"Hamilton, please untie us!"

said Ted.

"No way!" said Hamilton.

"If I untie you,

you will make me

leave my house."

"The Quimbys really miss you,"

said Ted.

"I miss them, too," said Hamilton.

"But they never

should have left me!"

And he disappeared.

Fred and Ted wriggled out of
the vacuum cleaner cord.
"I do not know why the Quimbys
miss Hamilton," said Fred.
"He is just upset," said Ted.

Fred picked up the vacuum cleaner
and the fishnet.

"I am going back to the truck,"
he said. "I give up!"

"I will try to talk
to Hamilton," said Ted.

"Maybe he will listen to me."

Ted wandered around the house

looking for Hamilton.

"Hamilton!" called Ted.

"Let's talk. I know you are upset."

But Hamilton did not answer.

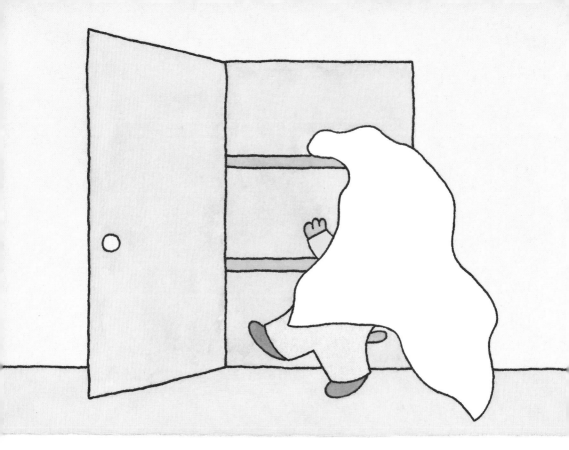

Ted came to a closet door.

"I wonder if Hamilton is in here,"

he said.

Ted opened the door.

An old sheet

that the Quimbys had left behind

fell on top of Ted.

"Help! I cannot see!" cried Ted.

He tried to get out

from under the sheet,

but he was all tangled up.

"Help me! Help me!" he shouted.

Just then Hamilton came into the room.

"Egads!" cried Hamilton.

"A ghost! *GET ME OUT OF HERE!*"

Hamilton flew out of the house and
right into the front seat
of Fred and Ted's truck.
"Hamilton! What are *you* doing here?"
asked Fred.
"I am scared," said Hamilton.
"There is a ghost in my house!"
"But you are a ghost," said Fred.
"Why are you scared?"

"That ghost is the scariest ghost

I have ever seen!" cried Hamilton.

"I want to move

to the Quimbys' new house

right now!"

"But where is Ted?" asked Fred.

"Who knows?" said Hamilton.

"Hamilton, you wait here," said Fred.

"I will go get Ted."

"Watch out for the ghost!"

said Hamilton.

Fred went back into the house.

"Ted! Ted! Where are you?"

called Fred.

"Help! Help!" cried Ted.

"Oh no!" said Fred.

"It's the new ghost!"

"It's me!" cried Ted. "Help me!"

"Ted! What happened?" asked Fred.

Fred lifted the sheet off of Ted.

"This sheet fell on top of me,"
said Ted.

"You sure scared Hamilton,"
said Fred.

"Where is Hamilton?" asked Ted.

"He is waiting in the truck,"
said Fred.

"He wants to move

to the Quimbys' new house."

Fred and Ted ran to the truck.

"Let's get out of here!"

cried Hamilton.

They drove to

the Quimbys' new house.

"Nice house!" said Hamilton.

"Hamilton!" cried the Quimbys.

"We missed you!"

"I hear that you guys

can't live *without* me,"

said Hamilton.

"So I guess I will

have to let you

live *with* me!"

Hamilton flew into the new house.

"Thank you, Fred and Ted,"

said Mr. Quimby.

"You did it!

You moved a ghost!"

"You really are the Mighty Movers!"

cried Mrs. Quimby.

"Big or small,

we move it all," said Fred.

"Whether firm or flighty," said Ted,

"call the Mighty!"